A Star Explodes

The Story of Supernova 1054

A STAR EXPLODES

The Story of Supernova 1054

Written by
James Gladstone

Illustrated by
Yaara Eshet

Owlkids Books

Long ago, a star exploded in our galaxy,

burning bright as billions of suns.

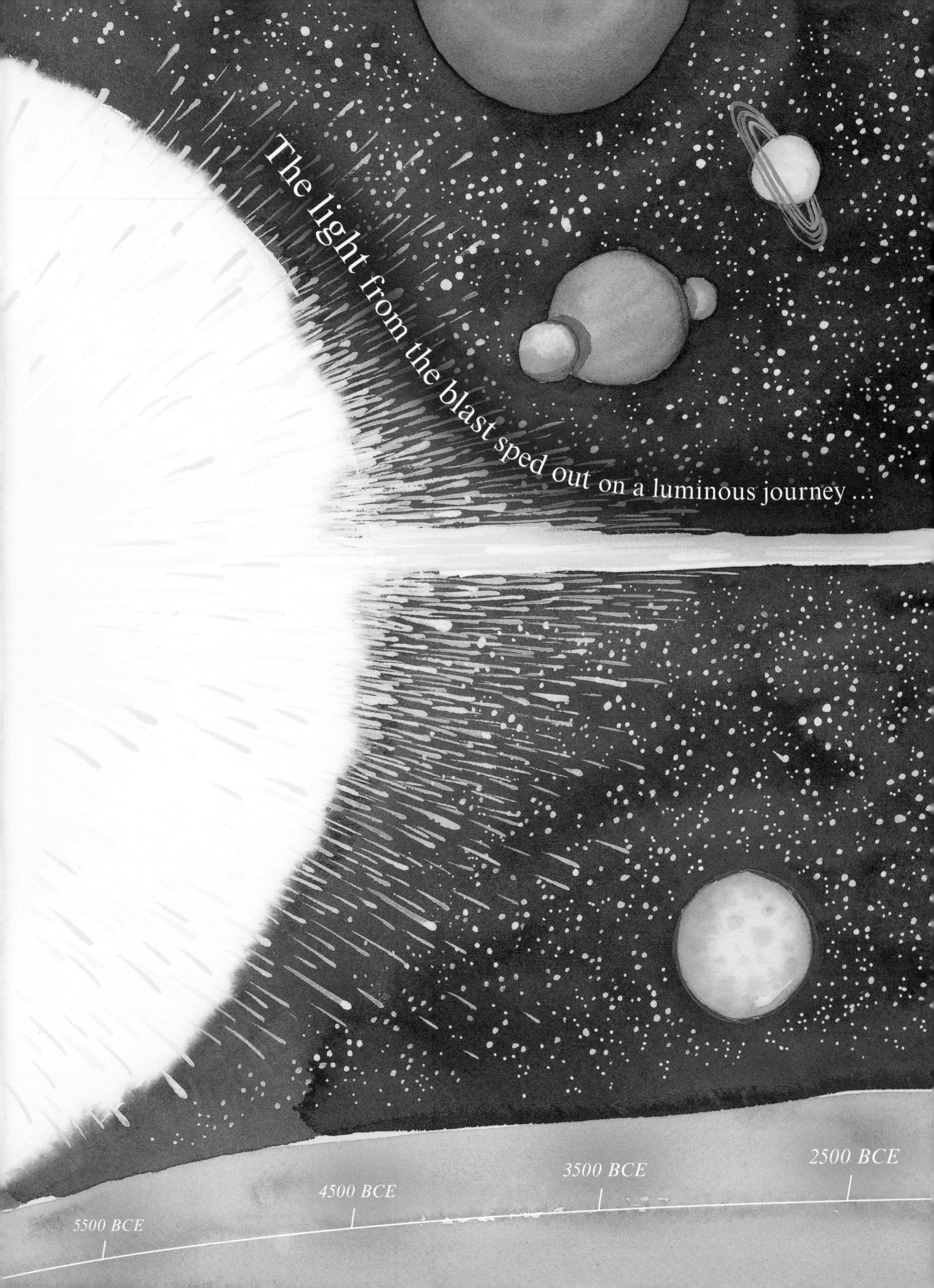

The light from the blast sped out on a luminous journey …

a journey that would last thousands of years.

Until one day, in the year 1054, that distant light arrived in Earth's morning sky.

A guest star—that's what the astronomer's daughter called it. Like a friend from out of nowhere, a new star had suddenly appeared.

In China, people of the emperor's court gazed in awe as the light of the guest star shone through the day.

At night, the young astronomer saw its light shine brighter than all the other stars.

And watching from the river bridge, she wondered, “Do other people in the world see the guest star’s shining gift of light?”

They did.

In time the light faded, and the world waved goodbye.
But were memories of this sky friend all that would remain?

If the young astronomer could have looked deeper into
the star fields of night, this is what she would have seen …

A nebula—a vast cloud of gas and dust—
was growing where the guest star used to be.

And as the nebula grew, our knowledge of the stars was growing too.

Centuries passed into the age of the telescope. It was as though a small light had been switched on in a dark room.

Astronomers could now see objects in deep space that no one before had seen.

One stargazer thought the nebula looked like a crab, and that's why we call it the Crab Nebula to this day.

Many years later, scientists learned that some huge stars explode. They called these star blasts supernovas.

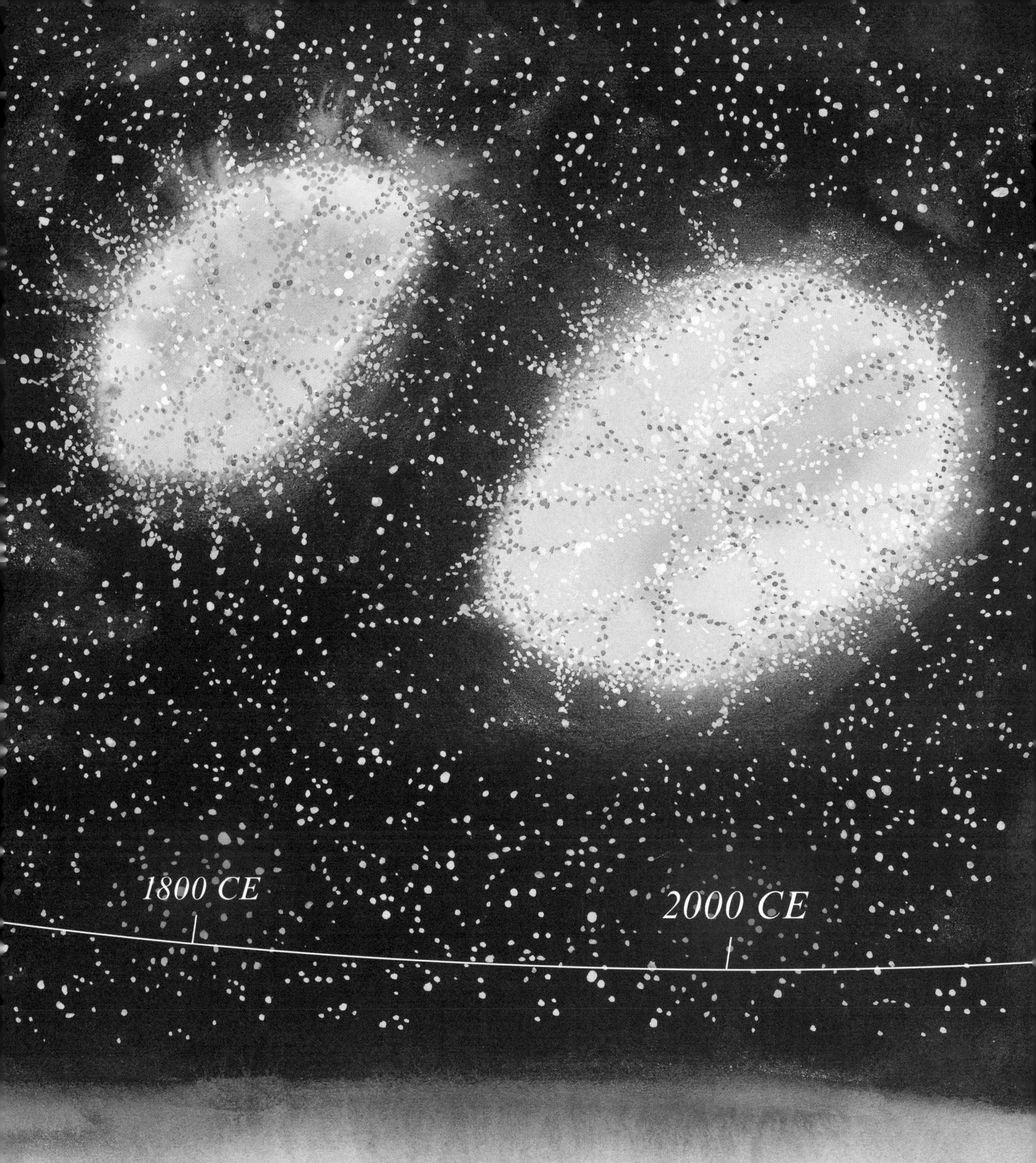

After a blast, a supernova leaves behind starry remains that, with time, spread farther throughout space.

So how did the guest star fit into this dark-sky puzzle?

The guest star was no star at all. It was the light of Supernova 1054—that long-ago explosion in space.

And the Crab Nebula is the starry remains of Supernova 1054.

The Crab Nebula is still growing today.

What's more—and what is so incredible—supernovas scatter their starry remains throughout the universe.

Some of those remains will become part of new worlds and new life yet to be.

Just as star remains from long ago are part of all things on our world …

… including you and me.

One day, you might see a supernova glow like a flame that warms a cool night.

And you may wonder,
"What worlds will grow from
this seed of light that shines
brighter than all the stars?"

WHAT IS A SUPERNOVA?

A supernova is a gigantic star explosion. The explosion is so big that, for a brief time, its light shines brighter than the billions of other stars in its galaxy. But supernovas are rare events, and most stars do not end their life cycles in this way. A galaxy may have only a few stars that go supernova each century. However, because there are billions of galaxies in the universe, astronomers may see many supernovas each year.

One type of supernova starts from a massive star—a star at least eight times bigger than our Sun. A star like this uses its fuel much faster than a smaller star. After a few million years, when a massive star runs out of fuel, gravity causes it to collapse in on itself. This sets off a huge explosion—a supernova.

Before a massive star goes supernova, it creates all kinds of elements like carbon, oxygen, and iron. When the star explodes, it blasts those elements into the universe, and some of them become part of planets, moons, and life—such as all life on Earth!

SUPERNOVA 1054

The massive star that became Supernova 1054 exploded about 7,500 years ago.* It took thousands of years for the light of Supernova 1054 to reach Earth. That's why people did not see its light until the year 1054. (Light travels faster than anything else in the universe. But the universe is so big that it takes starlight hundreds, thousands, even billions of years to reach our telescopes—and our eyes—on Earth.)

THE CRAB NEBULA

The starry remains of Supernova 1054—its gas and dust—make up what we now call the Crab Nebula. This nebula is known as a supernova remnant, and there are many other supernova remnants in the universe that astronomers study. The Crab Nebula is still getting bigger. It is expanding at a super-fast speed of about 930 miles (1,500 kilometers) per second! At that speed, you could circle our planet in about 27 seconds. (It would take the fastest jet airplane about 12 hours to go all the way around Earth.)

*The date of the explosion may change as scientists continue to research the Crab Nebula. And the speed of the expansion of the nebula may change with future research.

For young Henry and his mom — J.G.

To Yotam, Tamar, and Ran, my three stars — Y.E.

ACKNOWLEDGMENT: The author wishes to thank Paul A. Delaney, Professor Emeritus, Department of Physics and Astronomy, York University, Toronto, for his time and helpful feedback.

Owlkids Books acknowledges the financial support of the Canada Council for the Arts, the Ontario Arts Council, the Government of Canada through the Canada Book Fund (CBF), and the Government of Ontario through the Ontario Creates Book Initiative for our publishing activities.

Owlkids Books gratefully acknowledges that our office in Toronto is located on the traditional territory of many nations, including the Mississaugas of the Credit, the Chippewa, the Wendat, the Anishinaabeg, and the Haudenosaunee Peoples.

Published in Canada by Owlkids Books Inc.
1 Eglinton Avenue East, Toronto, ON, M4P 3A1

Published in the US by Owlkids Books Inc.
1700 Fourth Street, Berkeley, CA, 94710

Library of Congress Control Number: 2022937966

Library and Archives Canada Cataloguing in Publication

Title: A star explodes : the story of Supernova 1054 / written by James Gladstone ; illustrated by Yaara Eshet.
Names: Gladstone, James, 1969- author. | Eshet, Yaara (Illustrator), illustrator.
Identifiers: Canadiana 20220232334 | ISBN 9781771474986 (hardcover)
Subjects: LCSH: Supernova 1054—Juvenile literature. | LCSH: Crab Nebula—Juvenile literature.
Classification: LCC QB843.S95 S73 2023 | DDC j523.8/4465—dc23

Edited by Jennifer Stokes | Designed by Alisa Baldwin

Photo credit: page 31, courtesy of NASA

Manufactured in Guangdong Province, Dongguan City, China, in August 2022, by Toppan Leefung Packaging & Printing (Dongguan) Co., Ltd. Job #BAYDC116

A B C D E F

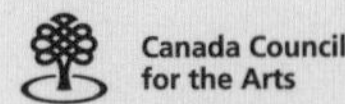

Canada